PINKY BLOOM AND THE CASE OF THE SILENT SHOFAR

PINKY BLOOM AND THE CASE OF THE SILENT SHOFAR

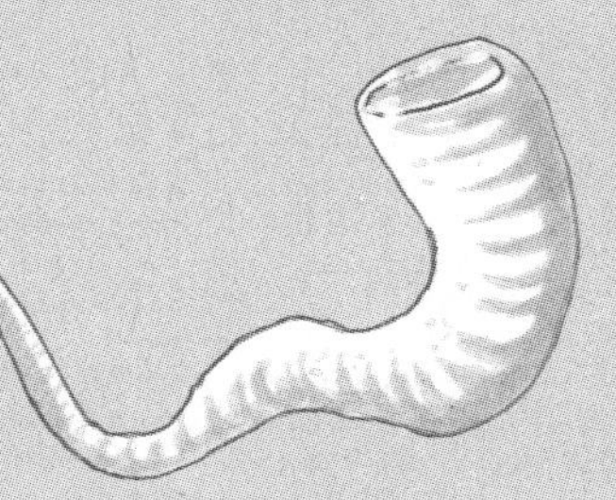

JUDY PRESS

ILLUSTRATED BY

ERICA-JANE WATERS

KAR-BEN PUBLISHING

KAR-BEN PUBLISHING®
An imprint of Lerner Publishing Group, Inc.
241 First Avenue North
Minneapolis, MN 55401 USA

Website address: www.karben.com

Main body text set in Bembo Std regular.
Typeface provided by Monotype Typography.

Library of Congress Cataloging-in-Publication Data

Names: Press, Judy, 1944– author. | Waters, Erica-Jane, illustrator.
Title: Pinky Bloom and the case of the silent shofar / Judy Press ; illustrated by Erica-Jane Waters.
Description: Minneapolis, MN : Kar-Ben Publishing, an imprint of Lerner Publishing Group, Inc., 2022. | Series: Pinky Bloom | Audience: Ages 8–12. | Audience: Grades 2–3. | Summary: Penina "Pinky" Bloom is starting a pet-sitting business, which means she has even more cases than usual on her plate: a missing pet, a suspicious pet shop employee, and her dad's strangely silent shofar.
Identifiers: LCCN 2021014676 | ISBN 9781728438948
Subjects: LCSH: Pet sitting—Juvenile fiction. | Guinea pigs—Juvenile fiction. | Wild animal trade—Juvenile fiction. | Shofar—Juvenile fiction. | Brothers and sisters—Juvenile fiction. | Jewish girls—Juvenile fiction. | Jewish families--Juvenile fiction. | Brooklyn (New York, N.Y.)—Juvenile fiction. | CYAC: Mystery and detective stories. | Pet sitting—Fiction. | Guinea pigs—Fiction. | Wild animal trade—Fiction. | Shofar—Fiction. | Brothers and sisters—Fiction. | Jews—United States—Fiction. | Brooklyn (New York, N.Y.)—Fiction.
Classification: LCC PZ7.P921927 Pk 2022 | DDC 813.54 [Fic]—dc23

LC record available at https://lccn.loc.gov/2021014676

Manufactured in the United States of America
1-49731-49634-10/28/2021

For my beloved aunt, Anne Spero
—J.P.

Chapter One

I, Penina "Pinky" Bloom, lover of all things that bark, meow, growl, hiss, purr, and squeak, am about to become the world's greatest pet sitter.

In case you're wondering, I'm still Brooklyn's greatest kid detective. No one said you can't do two things at once, like eating a bagel with one hand and petting my cat, D.J., with the other hand.

My idea for starting a pet sitting business came from my Grandma Phyllis. She visited last Passover and left her dog at home.

"Someone who takes care of pets put a sign up by

the mailboxes in my building," she told me. "I called, and now she's watching Bubeleh."

The week before Rosh Hashanah, I sat down at my computer and typed in *how to start your own business.* The results popped up a second later.

1. Have an idea. (Okay, I've got that. It's a pet sitting business.)
2. Make a business plan. (Check with Grandma to find out what Bubeleh's pet sitter charged.)
3. Make a marketing plan. (Huh? I'll need some help with this one.)
4. Let people know about your business. (I can post flyers and email all my friends.)
5. Get financing. (Mom and Dad???)
6. Find an office. (My room!)

Phew! There was so much to think about and a lot of work to do before I could even get started.

Someone knocked on my bedroom door. I had a feeling it was my brother, Avi. He's officially the most annoying second grader I've ever met.

"Avi, I'm busy with my marketing plan," I yelled through the door. "Go away and don't bother me."

"Pinky, it's me—Lucy. I have something important to tell you."

Lucy Chang lives two floors below me. I opened the door, and she rushed in. "I have exciting news! I got a pet guinea pig!"

A girl in my class has goldfish. And a boy in our building has a hamster. But I'd never known anyone with a pet pig!

Chapter Two

Lucy and I sat down together on my bed. "Pinky, do you remember when I said that I really, really, really wanted a pet?"

"Of course. You've said it a zillion times. It's the thing you want most in the world, even more than having a sleepover pizza party with our friends. But how did you decide to get a guinea pig for a pet?"

"They're really friendly and pretty easy to take care of," explained Lucy. She pulled out her phone. "Here's a picture of Mei-Mei. That's what I named her."

"Oh, she's so cute!" I said, looking at the picture. Mei-Mei had rounded ears, short legs, and no tail. Her fur was brown and tan with patches of white. "Are you going to take her to the pet show at the library next Sunday?"

"No, I can't," said Lucy. "I'm going to visit my auntie next weekend."

"Do you need a pet sitter? I'm starting my own pet sitting business. You could be my first customer."

"Wow, that's great!" said Lucy. "I'll definitely hire you to look after Mei-Mei. How much are you charging?"

I hadn't decided that yet. So I said, "Since you're my first client, I'll give you a discount. Your total will come to zero dollars."

"Thanks, Pinky! You can even take Mei-Mei to the pet show if you want."

I had planned to bring my cat, D.J., but I didn't think he'd mind missing the show this time. "You'll have to show me how to take care of her." I'd never looked after any animal except for D.J., but how hard could it be?

"Don't worry. I'll tell you everything you need to know. And I'll bring over her water bottle, a bag of bedding, some food pellets, her feeding dish, her hiding tunnel, her nail clipper, her grooming brush, and her carrier."

Wow, this was going to be more work than I'd thought!

"I actually have to go to the pet store on Friday after school to buy more bedding for her cage," Lucy added. "Do you want to go with me?"

"Sure! I'll just have to ask my parents for permission."

The door to my room opened again, and Avi marched in. "Pinky, if you go to the pet store, I'm going with you."

"This is between Lucy and me," I said. "And by the way, it's rude to listen in on other people's conversations."

Avi ignored this. "I'm getting a pet too," he announced. "And you'll never guess what kind."

"Are you making this up, Avi?" I said. "Like the time you told me you were entering the hot dog–eating contest at Coney Island?"

"This is for real, Pinky. Mom and Dad said I could get a pet because I got a perfect score on my spelling test. Come on—try to guess what it is!"

I wasn't sure I believed he was getting a pet at

all. I made a wild guess. "It's a vampire bat that you found in Prospect Park."

Lucy joined in. "I think you're getting a bearded dragon—one that looks like a dinosaur and breathes fire."

"Even better," said Avi. "It's a Madagascar hissing cockroach. They come from an island off of Africa, and they make hissing noises through the two tubes they use for breathing."

I blinked a few times. "Avi, did you say you're getting a *cockroach*?"

"That's right, Pinky. For your information, Madagascar hissing cockroaches make great pets. My friend Max already gave me his old terrarium, and I'm going to use my allowance for the other pet supplies."

That was all Brooklyn needed—another cockroach. And this one was going to live in my apartment!

Chapter Three

After Lucy went home, I helped get ready for dinner. My job was to make the salad. Avi was supposed to set the table, which didn't always happen.

As soon as I asked Mom about going to the pet store with Lucy on Friday afternoon, Avi burst into the kitchen and declared, "I'm going too!"

I gave him my evil eye. "No way, Avi. If you want to go, Mom or Dad can take you another time."

"You're not my boss, Pinky. I already asked Dad, and he's going to take us since he needs to buy more kitty litter for D.J."

We adopted D.J. from our local animal shelter. He's named for Derek Jeter, the greatest Yankee ever to play shortstop.

"You can *all* go to the pet store with Lucy," Mom chimed in. "Now, dinner's ready, so go sit down."

We were in the middle of eating when Mom told us that Grandma Phyllis was coming to visit for the holidays. Next week was the start of Rosh Hashanah, the Jewish New Year. That's when we go to synagogue to pray and hear the blowing of the shofar to welcome in the New Year. This year, my dad had been asked to blow the shofar in our synagogue on Rosh Hashanah, which is a big honor. I figured Grandma Phyllis wanted to see him do it.

When Grandma Phyllis is here, she sleeps in Avi's room, and I'm stuck with him in my room. Which might not be a problem if he didn't bring all his stuff with him. And if he didn't keep me awake with his snoring.

"Does Avi *have* to move into my room this time?" I said. "Can't he share a room with Grandma Phyllis? He can still use the blow-up mattress."

"Grandma Phyllis enjoys having a room to herself," Mom said. "Besides, she's bringing Bubeleh with her because the pet sitter wasn't available. She and the dog will need plenty of space."

Bubeleh is the most spoiled dog ever. She'll only eat organic, kosher dog food. And when she goes to the groomer, she gets her nails polished.

"You and Avi can work things out," Mom told me.

I looked over at Avi. He was grinning from ear to ear.

Chapter Four

On Friday after school, Dad, Avi, and I met up with Lucy and walked to the pet store a few blocks away. On our way there, we passed the Judaica shop, where we buy things we need for the Jewish holidays.

Dad peeked in the shop's window. "I see they've got a big collection of shofars," he said. "After we visit the pet store, I'll come back here to buy one."

"Dad, why do you need to buy a shofar?" I asked. "The synagogue already has one."

"That's true, Pinky. But it's a tough instrument to play, so I need one to practice with at home."

The shofar blasts remind us to ask forgiveness for the things we've done wrong. I could tell that Dad didn't want to mess up such an important job.

Avi was getting impatient. "Let's go!" he whined. "I want to buy the cockroaches."

I opened my eyes wide. "Avi, exactly how many cockroach*es* are you planning to buy?"

"I have to get more than one. I read that when there's a whole colony, they all hiss together."

If you ask me, even one cockroach is too many!

"I think two will be just fine, Avi," said Dad. "And make sure they're both boys so we don't end up with a large family of cockroaches!"

Inside Mr. Goldstein's pet store, there were shelves piled high with bags of dog and cat food, cat climbing poles, scratching posts, doggie beds, pet toys, and grooming supplies. I saw crates and kennels for puppies and kittens, tanks for lizards, and an aquarium full of colorful tropical fish.

Ava went straight to a glass tank swarming with huge, shiny, brown cockroaches. "Aren't they awesome, Pinky? Which one would you pick?"

I rolled my eyes and didn't say a word.

Dad went to get D.J.'s kitty litter, and Lucy started to look for Mei-Mei's bedding.

"Can I help you find something?" a store clerk asked us. His name tag said *Ziggy.*

While Lucy was busy telling Ziggy what she needed, I went off to explore the store on my own. I had some money saved from my allowance and thought that D.J. might like a toy mouse to chase around the house.

While I was looking around, I came to a closed door with a sign that said, *PRIVATE! Do Not Enter!*

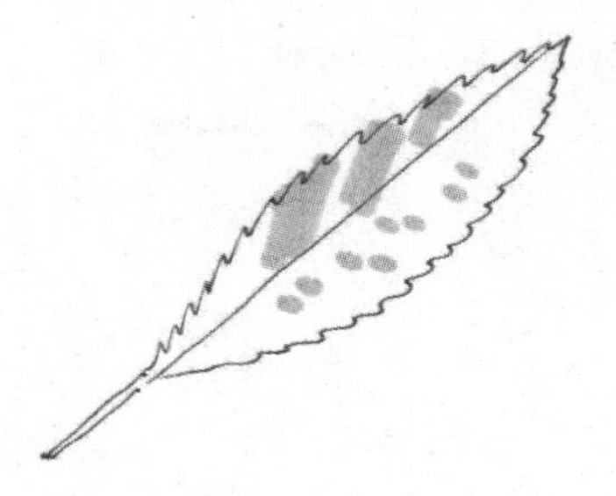

Chapter Five

Lying on the floor outside the door was a feather. I picked it up. It had tan and black stripes and a pointy quill. I'm not an expert, but judging by the size of it, I figured it must've fallen off a really large bird!

I was still holding the feather in my hand when Lucy came over. "Pinky, there you are," she said. "I found the bedding for Mei-Mei. What are you up to?"

I handed Lucy the feather. "Look what I found on the floor. Where do you think it came from?"

Lucy put down the bag of bedding she was carrying. "Um, I don't think the store sells any birds this big, but we can go see for ourselves."

We found Ziggy again. "Excuse me," I said. "Where do you keep your birds?"

"Over here." He led us into a side room full of big birdcages. All kinds of birds sat on perches, chirping at each other. I compared their feathers to the one I'd found. None of them matched.

Ziggy narrowed his eyes at me. "What's that you're holding?"

"A feather I found on the floor. Do you know what bird it came from?"

Ziggy snatched the feather out of my hand and put it in his pocket. "Probably just a pigeon feather."

There are a zillion pigeons in New York. I know a pigeon feather when I see one, and the feather I'd found definitely belonged to a much bigger bird. But before I could say so, Ziggy stormed away. He looked annoyed—or maybe worried.

Lucy looked at her phone. "I have to go. My dad just texted me. We need to pack for the weekend trip. I'll drop Mei-Mei off with you later today."

Lucy left, and I went to find my family. My dad was at the checkout counter, paying Mr. Goldstein for D.J.'s kitty litter. Avi stood next to him, holding a shopping bag in one hand and a small plastic container in the other.

"You should be all set," Mr. Goldstein was telling Avi. "You've got wood chips and a heat lamp for your terrarium, food and water dishes, and pellet food. You can also feed your cockroaches fresh fruits and vegetables."

"Pinky, do you want to meet my cockroaches?" asked Avi. He held up the container, which had tiny air holes poked in the top and sides.

"Thanks, but no thanks, Avi. You'd better make sure that lid's on tight and they don't escape."

"Don't worry. Ziggy put them inside, and he said they can't get out. At least until I move them to the terrarium at home."

"Ugh. Great." I had a bad feeling about those cockroaches.

"Let's get going," Dad said. "We have to stop by the Judaica shop on the way home. I'm anxious to get that shofar."

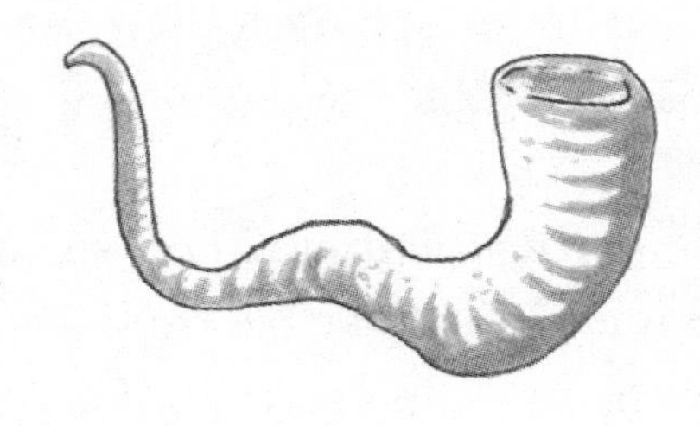

Chapter Six

The Judaica shop was crowded with people getting ready for the high holidays. The shop sells everything from Kiddush cups and menorahs to yarmulkes and gifts made in Israel. When we walked in, Mr. Simon, the owner, was talking to a few people next to a glass display case.

"Welcome, Bloom family," he said. He belongs to our synagogue and is a friend of my dad's. "I've been showing these customers something special. You should take a look."

Inside the display case were rows of watches with

Hebrew numbers on the dials.

My mom wears a watch that tells her how many steps she walked that day. And when I was six, Grandma Phyllis bought me a princess watch for my birthday. But I'd never seen a watch with Hebrew numbers.

Mr. Simon reached into the case and took out one of the watches. "In the old days, a watch like this would have had a chain that clipped to a buttonhole," he explained. "Then the wearer tucked it inside a pants pocket or a vest."

"Do people still buy these watches?" Dad asked Mr. Simon. "I've never seen anyone wear one."

"I sell a few. Some people like them because they remember that their grandfathers or great-grandfathers once wore pocket watches like these. Could I interest you in one?"

"Thanks, but I'd like to buy a shofar," Dad replied. "I've been asked to blow it at Rosh Hashanah services."

"Mazel tov," Mr. Simon said. He put the watch back in the case. "You've come to the right place. I'll let Hannah Cohen help you find the right shofar for you."

I didn't know it at the time, but that was the start of a new mystery I was going to solve!

of JEWISH HOLIDAYS
of JEWISH HOLIDAYS
Book of JEWISH
Book of JEWISH
Book of JEWISH

Chapter Seven

Hannah Cohen goes to my school, but she's a lot older than I am. Her younger sister, Rebecca, is in my class.

"I'd be happy to show you the shofars," Hannah told my dad. "Do you have something particular in mind?"

Avi set down his container and his bag of pet supplies so he could pick up a shofar that was extra-long and curvy. He put it up to his mouth and pretended to blow into the narrow end. "I want Dad to buy this one," he declared.

I found a shofar that was decorated with pictures of Jerusalem and the Old City. "This is my favorite," I said. "The pictures are great."

Dad examined every shofar Hannah handed him and tried playing each one. We watched as he put his mouth around the narrow end, puffed up his cheeks, and blew through the opening. The sounds he blew were *womp, womp, womp* instead of *tekiah, tekiah, tekiah, tekiah.*

"Keep trying, Mr. Bloom," Hannah said. "Blow in a small amount of dry air, and don't pucker your cheeks. The power of your breaths should come from your diaphragm."

Avi tugged on my sleeve. "Pinky, this is getting boring. Can we go back to the pet store? I want to buy a whistle to help me train my cockroaches. I still have enough money from my allowance. Please?"

I looked over at Dad. He was taking his time choosing a shofar. Since I had forgotten to buy the toy mouse for D.J., I said, "Okay, Avi. But I have my doubts that cockroaches are trainable."

"Don't be long," Dad told us on our way out the door. "I'm almost done choosing a shofar."

Avi and I walked back to the pet store. In front of the building, Ziggy was loading crates into the pet store's van. He was also talking into a wireless earpiece. "Yeah, meet me in the parking lot. I do a lot of business there—buying *and* selling. Nobody there ever suspects anything."

I leaned closer to see what was inside the van. I caught a glimpse of a cage, but it was covered with a cloth, so I couldn't tell what was in it.

Ziggy turned and noticed us. "Don't you kids have somewhere else to be?"

That's when I heard a noise coming from the cage in the van. It sounded like wings fluttering, along with a high-pitched squeaking.

I wondered if it could be the bird whose feather I'd found inside the store. "Ziggy, can you show us what's in that cage?" I politely asked.

"No," he snapped. "Get lost. Can't you see I'm busy?"

I thought that Ziggy needed to learn some manners!

"Let's go, Pinky," Avi said, tugging on my sleeve. "Dad said to hurry."

I knew Avi was right. But the detective in me wished we could stick around. I was pretty sure Ziggy was hiding something in his van that he didn't want us to see.

Chapter Eight

After we bought Avi's whistle and D.J.'s mouse, Avi and I headed back to the Judaica shop. Dad was blowing into another shofar. It sounded almost like a real *Tekiaaaaah*. "I like this one," he said.

Mr. Simon hurried over. "I found a shofar that's nearly the same as that one but a little nicer," he said. "It was in the storage room." He held out a long shofar that curled upward. It looked almost exactly like the one Dad had been practicing with.

Hannah had a worried look on her face. "Mr.

Simon, I don't think that shofar is right for Mr. Bloom," she said. "I think he likes the one I just showed him."

Suddenly, someone yelled, "Eeeek, I saw a cockroach! It crawled across the floor and made a hissing noise!"

I looked over at the spot where Avi had set his plastic container. The lid was slightly open. I groaned.

"Don't be afraid," Avi said. "It's my pet Madagascar hissing cockroach, and it won't hurt anybody because it doesn't bite. It'll also be easy to catch because it's three whole inches long."

A few people panicked and ran out of the store. Other customers helped us search for Avi's cockroach. They looked inside Kiddush cups and tzedakah boxes, under matzo covers, and behind a display of T-shirts that said *New York Yankees* in Hebrew.

After a minute, I found Avi's cockroach hiding under a display case in a corner of the store. "Over here!" I called out.

Avi scooped up the cockroach and put it back into the container. Then he apologized to Mr. Simon for the trouble.

SPECIAL OFFER
BOOK of JEWISH HOLIDAYS
Book of JEWISH HOLID
Book of JEWISH HOLI
Book of JEWISH HOLI

"I guess I'd better buy that shofar and get out of here before disaster strikes again!" said Dad. "Thank you for helping me pick the right one, Hannah. I'm going to take it home and practice what you taught me to do."

Hannah went off to wrap the shofar. "She's one of our best salespeople," said Mr. Simon. "Her family once owned this store, though that was many years ago."

On the way home, Avi said, "Look! There's Madame Olga!" He pointed across the street at a lady dressed in a long, flowery skirt. "Let's say hi."

Madame Olga is a part-time babysitter and a full-time psychic who helps out when I'm on a case.

"Shabbat shalom, Bloom family," Madame Olga said when we got closer. "A beautiful day for a walk. Pinky, darling, tell me what's new. Have you solved any mysteries lately?"

"I've been busy with my new business," I answered. "I'm a pet sitter now."

"Exciting news! What are you calling your business?"

"Oh—I haven't picked a name yet." Maybe that was supposed to be part of the marketing plan.

"She's bringing Lucy's guinea pig to the pet

show at the library tomorrow," Avi interrupted. He turned to Dad. "Please, please, please can I bring my cockroaches to the pet show?"

"Just make sure they don't escape again," Dad cautioned.

The pet show happens every year. Pet owners bring their dogs, cats, hamsters, rabbits, and guinea pigs. But NO ONE has ever brought a pet cockroach!

Chapter Nine

When we got home, I went straight to my room. My pet sitting business needed a name! So I grabbed a paper and a pencil and wrote down a few ideas:

- Tails & Scales Pet Sitting (Nice rhyme, but not quite right)
- Cute Critters Pet Sitter (What if they're *not* cute?)
- The Handy Dandy Pet Minder (Too many words)
- Woof & Meow Pet Sitting (Some pets don't woof or meow)

I was in the middle of trying to choose a name when Avi walked in. "Pinky, I know what we can call our pet sitting business."

"Avi, you and I are not going into business together. Period, end of story."

"But I came up with the perfect name!"

I took in a deep breath and let it out slowly. "Okay, I'm listening. What is it?"

"Pinky Bloom, Pet Sitter."

Hmm. It was simple and easy to remember, and it had a nice ring to it! "Thanks, Avi. I like it. But that still doesn't mean you and I are partners."

"What if I'm a silent partner, Pinky? I can be quiet and only talk when I have something important to say."

Before I could answer, the doorbell rang. I ran to get it, hoping it was Lucy bringing over Mei-Mei.

"It's me!" Grandma Phyllis sang out. "I'm early for the holidays, but I'm here in time for Shabbat."

As we all stood in the doorway hugging Grandma Phyllis, I felt something tickle my feet. I looked down and saw Bubeleh. She was licking my toes!

D.J. sneaked out from under the living room couch. He slowly made his way over to Bubeleh, who took one look at my cat and drooled gobs of saliva on our new carpet.

"I'll put your things in Avi's room," Mom said, helping Grandma with her suitcase. "He can move into Pinky's room after dinner."

Rosh Hashanah was in five days. Yom Kippur was ten days after that. Which meant Avi and I would be roommates for the next fifteen days, ten hours, twenty minutes, and two seconds. Not that I was counting!

"Would you like to see my new shofar?" Dad asked Grandma Phyllis. "It's not time for Shabbat yet, so I can give you a demonstration."

"Take a seat, everyone," Mom said. "Dad's performance is about to begin."

"Don't expect too much," Dad said. "I still need lots of practice before I get it right."

He wrapped two hands around the shofar, making sure to hold it with the curl upright. Then he pressed his lips against the opening and gently blew into the mouthpiece.

We waited, expecting to hear the shofar make a long, low *Tekiaaaaah* . . .

But the shofar was completely silent!

Dad's face turned red. "Let me try again," he said. He puffed up his cheeks and blew into the shofar. It still didn't make a sound. "I don't get it," said Dad. "The shofar made plenty of noise when I played it at the shop. I guess I'll have to take it back and exchange it for one that works."

I wondered what could have made the shofar stop working. I've solved a lot of mysteries, but I'd never heard of a silent shofar before.

Chapter Ten

There was a knock on the front door. I jumped up from the couch and ran to see who was there.

"Who is it?" I said, standing on tiptoes and squinting through the peephole.

"It's Lucy. Is it okay if I drop Mei-Mei off now? I hope it's not Shabbat yet."

I slipped off the chain and opened the door. She was holding a cage in both hands and had a big bag slung over her shoulder. "We still have some time," I told her. "We don't light the candles until eighteen minutes before sundown."

Mom was in the living room setting out the Shabbat candles. "Hello, Lucy," she said. "Pinky is so excited to take care of Mei-Mei while you're away."

"I'm happy she can help out," Lucy said. "My auntie is celebrating her ninetieth birthday, and everyone in my family will be there."

Lucy carried Mei-Mei's cage into my room. It fit on top of my chest of drawers. "You can put the rest of her things in my closet," I said. "Just move the pile of dirty clothes on the floor."

The terrarium with Avi's cockroaches was on my desk, and D.J. was curled napping on my bed. With Mei-Mei here too, my room was starting to look like the Bronx Zoo!

I walked up to Mei-Mei's cage and peeked inside. I saw her water bottle, a cardboard tube, and her food dish. "Lucy, where is she? I don't see her."

"She's hiding in the tube," Lucy said. "Guinea pigs are shy, but they're also very curious. Give her a minute, and she'll come out to look for food."

I grabbed some paper and pencil and wrote down everything Lucy said about how to take good care of Mei-Mei.

"Fill the water bottle that's on the side of her

cage twice a day. And clean the cage and change the bedding daily."

I wrinkled my nose. Cleaning poop was going to be my least favorite part of the job.

"She can have small amounts of parsley, broccoli, carrots, and hay," Lucy said. "But remember, never feed a guinea pig chocolate or popcorn."

"Don't worry," I told her. "I've got this covered."

I was officially a pet sitter!

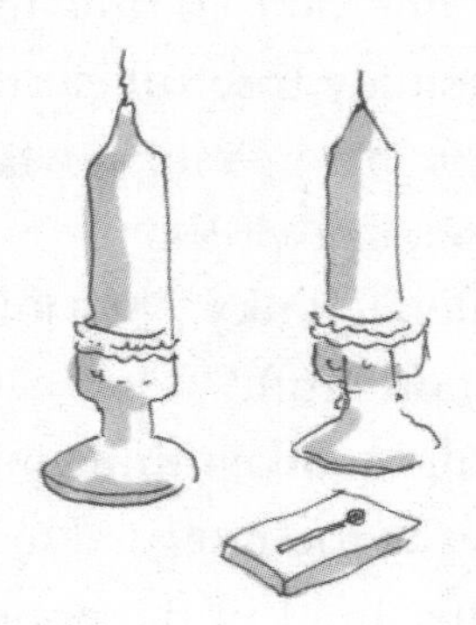

Chapter Eleven

I walked Lucy to the door. My dad was in the living room talking on the phone. " . . . seems like something's wrong with the shofar I bought this afternoon. I'd like to exchange it for another one as soon as possible. Please give me a call back when you get this message."

Dad put the phone down. "The Judaica shop is closed for the weekend. I left a voice mail for Mr. Simon, but I probably won't be able to get a new shofar until Monday."

I felt sorry for Dad. Rosh Hashanah was next

week, and he still didn't have a shofar to blow.

I got back to my room in time to see Avi bringing in a pair of muddy baseball cleats, his superhero pajamas, his New York Yankees backpack, and a book about poisonous reptiles.

"I'm almost done, Pinky," he said. "I just have to bring in a little more stuff."

"Do not bring another thing into my room!" I yelled. "It's already too crowded in here."

Mom stuck her head in the doorway. "Time to light."

After Mom lit the Shabbat candles and all the blessings were said, Grandma Phyllis said, "Avi, tell me about your new pet."

"There are two of them, Grandma. I named one Mazel, and the other is Tov. I'm taking them to the library pet show on Sunday. Bubeleh can come too!"

"What a wonderful idea." Grandma Phyllis bent down and fed Bubeleh a scrap of kosher chicken. Bubeleh drooled all over the floor. I was glad I was pet sitting for Mei-Mei and not for my grandmother's dog!

Chapter Twelve

Shabbat ended when we saw three stars in the sky on Saturday night. Dad made a blessing over the wine, and we passed around a spice container filled with sweet-smelling cloves. Next, he lit a braided havdalah candle that had three wicks. We held up our hands to see the reflection on our nails, and he said a blessing for us to have a good week.

Now that the Sabbath was over, I had to work on my business plan. So far, taking care of Mei-Mei had been easy-peasy. I figured I was ready to take my business to the next level.

Avi was sitting at my desk holding a pen. "Pinky, how do you spell *conscientious*?" he said. "Does it have one *c* or two?"

"Why do you want to know?"

"Because I'm working on our flyer. It's going to say that we're conscientious pet sitters."

"*Our* flyer, Avi?" I crossed my arms. "Since when did I give you permission to make a flyer about my business?"

Avi had on his sad face. "I was only trying to help."

I sighed. "Well, let me see what you've written. I might have to make some changes."

Avi handed over a piece of paper. Across the top in bold letters, he'd written *Avi and Pinky Bloom: Consheeinshish Pet Sitters.*

I took out a red pencil like the one my teacher, Mrs. Goldblum, uses to correct our papers. I changed the sign to *Pinky Bloom: Pet Sitter & Avi Bloom: Assistant Pet Sitter.* Then I added our phone number so people could contact us if they wanted to hire us.

"I can make more that look just like that," Avi offered. "And I can pass them out for you at the pet show."

Maybe having Avi for an assistant wouldn't be so bad. "Fine, go ahead."

Avi took out more paper and got to work. "Pinky, did you know that hissing cockroaches can climb up the glass walls of an aquarium and escape?"

"Thanks for letting me know, Avi. Your cockroaches had better not crawl into my bed when I'm asleep. Now please stop bugging me. I need peace and quiet to concentrate on my business plan. I don't want to hear another sound."

That made me think about Dad's shofar. Why didn't it make a sound? Had someone done something to damage it? Maybe it had been sabotaged!

I took out my detective notebook and started a new case entry. Under *SUSPECTS*, I wrote, *Mr. Simon???*

But Mr. Simon had no motive for selling Dad a silent shofar. In fact, as far as I knew, nobody had a motive for sabotaging Dad's shofar.

This case was going to be hard to crack!

Chapter Thirteen

The next morning, I took Mei-Mei out of her cage and ran a small brush through her tangled fur. "You're going to be the best-looking pet at the show," I whispered.

Mei-Mei made a squeaking noise. Lucy had told me that when guinea pigs make that sound, it means they're happy.

When I was done grooming Mei-Mei, I gently put her inside her travel carrier, which I'd lined with old newspaper. Then I added a cardboard tube so she would have a place to hide. I zipped the carrier closed and went into the kitchen to eat breakfast.

Grandma Phyllis was already there. "Pinky, darling," she said, "help me decide what Bubeleh should wear to the pet show."

In one hand, she was holding a tiny ballerina outfit for a dog. In the other hand was a dog's coat with tiny pink hearts.

Bubeleh is better dressed than any kid I know, including me. "I'm sure she'll look great in whatever she wears," I told Grandma Phyllis.

"Okay—the tutu it is!" she exclaimed. "Now I just have to find a leash that'll go with the outfit."

In a corner of the kitchen, Bubeleh was noisily chomping on her dog food. She couldn't care less what outfit Grandma Phyllis picked for her to wear!

When I was done eating my cereal, I grabbed a bottle of water and a handful of parsley from the fridge. The show would last a couple of hours, and I didn't want Mei-Mei to get hungry or thirsty.

Avi came into the kitchen with his backpack. "I put the cockroaches back in the plastic container, and I made sure the lid is extra tight this time," he said. "Now I just need to pack their food and a cotton ball soaked with water. That's what they drink if they get thirsty."

"Well, hurry up," I told him. "Mom's bringing the car around."

My dad had an important meeting at the synagogue, so he wasn't joining us. As soon as Avi had put a bag of apples, peppers, and carrots in his backpack for his cockroaches' lunch, we were ready to go. Grandma Phyllis, Avi, and I took the elevator down to the lobby. Mom was waiting with the car in front of our building.

Avi and I climbed into the backseat. I put Mei-Mei's carrier on the floor between my feet, and Avi held the container with the cockroaches on his lap.

"Bubeleh can sit between the two of you," Grandma Phyllis said as she got into the front passenger seat. "Riding in the car gives her a case of the *shpilkes*—nerves."

"I'm smooshed," Avi complained. "Move over, Pinky. You're taking up too much room."

"I can't, Avi! Why don't you move closer to the window?"

Mom turned around. "Settle down, you two! We'll be there before you know it."

Then Bubeleh let out a big, smelly fart! As far as I was concerned, we couldn't get to the library soon enough.

Chapter Fourteen

The Brooklyn Public Library is a two-story building made of brick and stone. There's a big open space in front of the main steps. That's where the pet show happens. This year, there were booths on the lawn and food stalls off to the side.

"Everyone out," Mom said as she drove the car up to the curb. "I'll park and then come find you."

A crowd had already gathered in front of the library. Ms. Maxwell, the head librarian, stood on the steps holding a microphone. "Welcome to our annual pet show, everyone," she said. "The Pet

Parade is about to start. All dogs should be on leashes. Walk around the outside of the building along with your pets. Then we'll meet back here on the lawn for the rest of our program."

I held tight to Mei-Mei's carrier as we did the Pet Parade. Avi and Grandma Phyllis were right behind us. Avi passed out all the flyers he'd made for my pet sitting business.

Afterward, we met up with Mom and went to a booth to hear a talk about therapy pets. Avi raised his hand and asked the speaker if his Madagascar hissing cockroaches would qualify.

"Dogs and cats are most commonly used in pet therapy," the speaker said. "But fish, guinea pigs, horses, and other animals that meet screening criteria can also be used."

Our next stop was the craft table, where we made toys for the animals at our local animal shelter. Ms. Feldman, the shelter's director, explained how shelters rescue stray animals and try to find new homes for them. "We have dogs, cats, and a variety of small animals like mice, rats, and rabbits. And we're always looking for volunteers to help with their care."

"What about snakes?" someone asked.

"Reptiles usually go to a special rescue center. There are lots of rescue centers for different types of animals, including exotic animals that aren't supposed to be kept as pets. Sometimes, people sell those animals illegally. But most of us wouldn't know how to take good care of them. That's why our shelter sticks to mammals."

"Can we get a dog?" Avi asked Mom. "I really want one!"

"I think we have enough pets in the house already," Mom said firmly.

Just then, Hannah Cohen hurried up to us. "Mrs. Bloom! I have to talk to you. It's very important."

"Nice to see you, Hannah," said Mom. "My husband mentioned that you helped him buy a shofar at the Judaica shop yesterday."

"There's been a mistake with the shofar Mr. Bloom took home," Hannah said. "I can come get it this afternoon. And I can bring over a replacement tomorrow when the shop reopens for the week."

"That's so kind," said Mom. "But you might as well wait to come get the old shofar until the store is open, so you can give him a new one at the same time. That way you won't have to stop by our apartment twice."

"Oh, it's really no trouble," said Hannah. Then she added in a hurry, "Actually, I have a key to the shop, so I can get a new shofar from there today. Would later this afternoon work?"

"Well, if you insist," said Mom. "My husband will be glad to get a new shofar as soon as possible. The holidays will be here shortly, and he has to practice."

Hannah looked so relieved that I started to wonder why she was so anxious to exchange the shofars. She wasn't even going to wait until the store opened! Mr. Simon had said she was one of his best salespeople, but most salespeople don't make deliveries to customers' homes.

I was starting to form a theory about the silent shofar. But I needed a little more time to figure everything out.

Chapter Fifteen

It was time for the picnic on the library's front lawn. We filled up plates with food, and Mom spread out the blanket she had brought. Grandma Phyllis and Bubeleh left to talk to a friend she knew from when she'd lived in Brooklyn.

I lifted Mei-Mei out of her carrying case so I could feed her some parsley, but she seemed more interested in the fruit and vegetables on our plates.

Avi unzipped his backpack. "It's time for my cockroaches to have their lunch too," he said.

"As long as I don't have to watch them eat,"

I said. "That'll spoil my appetite."

Suddenly, Grandma Phyllis rushed over. "It's Bubeleh!" she shouted. "She got stung by a bee! What if she's allergic? Should I take her to the vet?"

Mom pulled out her phone and scrolled through some search results. "Okay, it says here to brush away the bee's stinger, then apply a cold compress."

I noticed an ice-cream cart nearby. "I'll ask for some ice to put on Bubeleh's paw."

I sprinted over to the cart and told the ice-cream seller what had happened. He gave me an ice cube. I raced back and handed it to Grandma Phyllis. She applied the ice to Bubeleh's paw. Bubeleh whimpered a little, but she seemed more bothered by the cold ice than by the beesting.

All this only took a few seconds, but when I sat back down on the blanket, Mei-Mei was gone!

I frantically looked around. I checked inside the carrier, then searched the grass near where we were sitting.

"Mei-Mei's gone!" I cried. "Everyone, you have to help me look for her."

"Don't worry, darling," Grandma Phyllis said. "We'll find her. She couldn't have gotten far."

Mom dropped down on her hands and knees. "Guinea pigs have short legs," she said. "They don't move as fast as hamsters."

"I read about a guinea pig that ran ten meters in 8.81 seconds for a world record," Avi offered.

My voice was quivering. "We have to find Mei-Mei! Lucy will be so upset if I've lost her!"

"Let's split up," Grandma Phyllis suggested. "I'll look over by the food stalls. Avi, check those bushes near the parking lot."

"I'll walk around and ask if anyone has seen a guinea pig," said Mom.

Soon, Mom got a bunch of people to help us look for Mei-Mei. I tried to stay calm, but my hands were shaking and my heart was beating really fast. It felt like I was riding the roller coaster at Coney Island!

Avi ran over to me. "Pinky, you'll never guess what I saw."

"Tell me you saw Mei-Mei!"

"No—I saw a boa constrictor, just like the kind that's in the Bronx Zoo."

"Oh no!" I screamed. "Don't they eat small animals like GUINEA PIGS?"

"Don't worry, Pinky. Maybe it already ate its dinner."

I dropped down on the blanket. I was turning out to be a complete failure as a pet sitter!

ANNUAL PET SHOW
BROOKLYN LIBRARY

Chapter Sixteen

Eventually, we had to go home. Mom and Grandma Phyllis needed to do the holiday shopping. But I got Mom's permission to visit Madame Olga.

"Take your brother with you," Mom said. "Your dad won't be back for another hour."

Madame Olga works out of a storefront a block away from my home. The sign in her window used to say *Madame Olga, Spiritual Advisor and Psychic to Famous People*. But she must've changed it recently because now it said, *Madame Olga, Spiritual Advisor and Finder of Lost Items*. That was probably because she'd helped me with my last couple of cases. Now I really hoped she could help me find Mei-Mei.

I knocked and waited a few seconds. When there was no answer, I knocked again.

"I'm coming, I'm coming . . ." Madame Olga finally opened the door. "Pinky and Avi! Come in. I just baked a fresh babka. You'll take a slice."

"We need your help, Madame Olga," I said.

"Pinky lost Lucy's guinea pig," Avi added.

Madame Olga held her hands to her head. "So this is not such good news. Tell me what happened."

I told her about the picnic and how I had left Mei-Mei alone on the blanket. "When I got back, she was gone."

"You looked everywhere. So what did you find?" Madame Olga asked.

"I saw a boa constrictor," Avi volunteered. "And Ziggy from the pet store was there too."

I stared at Avi. "Why didn't you tell me he was there?"

"You never asked me, Pinky."

"What was he doing?"

"Just hanging around by the bushes in the parking lot."

Hmmm . . .

"Here's what we'll do," Madame Olga said. "We'll go to the animal shelter to see if someone brought a guinea pig there."

"That's a great idea," I said. I really hoped Mei-Mei would be at the shelter.

But if she wasn't, I had an idea for where to look next.

Chapter Seventeen

The animal shelter was a big building not far from the library. The lobby's walls were covered with photos of dogs, cats, and rabbits. One cat even looked like D.J.

"Welcome," said a woman behind a counter. "I'm Mrs. Howard. How can I help you?"

Madame Olga explained, "We're searching for a lost guinea pig and hoping someone brought it to the shelter."

Mrs. Howard studied her computer. "Looks like we have one! Follow me."

She led us down a long hallway. Along the walls were cages filled with barking dogs who wagged their tails as we walked by. Avi stopped in front of each cage, and I knew he was thinking about how much he wanted to adopt a dog.

"This is where we keep our smaller animals," Mrs. Howard said as we walked into a room. Cages with rabbits lined one wall. Some were asleep, and others were happily nibbling on green leaves.

"Here's our guinea pig." Mrs. Howard pointed to a smaller cage on the opposite wall. "Is this who you're looking for?"

I bent down to get a closer look. The guinea pig was mostly white with patches of brown around its ears.

My heart sank. "It's not Mei-Mei," I admitted. "She's tan and brown with patches of white."

"I know you're disappointed," Mrs. Howard said kindly. "Let me have a phone number where I can reach you, and I'll let you know if we get another guinea pig."

We thanked Mrs. Howard and told her we hoped all the animals at the shelter would get adopted.

"Can we go to the pet store next?" I asked. "It's not far."

"Isn't it closed on Sunday?" asked Madame Olga.

"Yes, but I have a feeling that Ziggy's still working. And I'd like to ask him some questions."

When we passed the library, we saw the pet store van in the parking lot. "Look!" cried Avi, pointing. "What if Ziggy found Mei-Mei and put her in the van?"

The rear doors of the van were wide open. I looked around, but I didn't see Ziggy. There were plenty of other cars in the parking lot, though. I remembered that Ziggy had said, "Meet me in the parking lot" in his phone call the other day. He'd also said, "Nobody there ever suspects anything."

I definitely suspected something now, even if I wasn't exactly sure what.

Before we could stop him, Avi ran over to the van.

"Avi! Come back!" I yelled.

Madame Olga and I raced after him. But he climbed right into the back of the van.

"Get out of there, Avi!" I shouted. "This isn't a game."

When he didn't answer, Madame Olga and I scrambled into the van. Avi was crouching down next to an empty cage, picking up a bird feather from the floor. It looked a lot like the feather I'd found at the pet store. "Mei-Mei's not in here," said Avi. "But look at this giant feather."

"Something's odd about this," said Madame Olga. "What is a pet store van doing in the library parking lot?" She pulled out her phone. I figured she was about to call one of our parents.

Suddenly, we heard footsteps coming toward the van. I turned around just in time to see Ziggy staring at us. He looked the way I felt when Avi invaded my room.

Before any of us could say anything, he slammed the van's rear doors shut. We were trapped inside!

Madame Olga ran to the doors and tried to open them, but it was no use. The engine started, and the van took off. It moved so fast that we all lost our balance. Madame Olga's phone flew out of her hand and crashed onto the floor. "Sit down!" she told us. "Brace yourselves!" Avi and I huddled in a corner of the van as it zoomed along, bumping over potholes.

After what seemed like a long time, the van came to a stop.

"Okay, ride's over," Ziggy said as he opened the doors. "You can get out now."

DOG BISCUITS
CAT BISCUITS
CAT BISCUITS

The van was parked by the pet store. "Young man, you're not very nice," Madame Olga said. "I should tell your mother."

"You kidnapped us!" yelled Avi.

"I didn't plan on that," snapped Ziggy. "But I couldn't let you ruin the business deal I'm about to make. Now get inside."

He pushed us into the store, which was empty. He opened the door marked *Private! Do Not Enter!* and shooed us inside.

"I'm hungry, and my parents are going to be mad, so you have to let us go home," Avi said.

"Put a sock in it!" Ziggy growled.

"Put a what in what?" said Avi.

Ziggy rolled his eyes. "I mean stop talking. I'll be back to let you out after I'm finished doing what I need to do." I wasn't sure I believed him. He turned and left the room. Then we heard the click of the door lock.

We were trapped in the pet store, and there was no way out!

Chapter Eighteen

"Stay calm," said Madame Olga. "My phone's acting funny since I dropped it in the van, but once I get it working right again, I'll call for help."

The room we were in wasn't very big. A desk sat near a tiny window, and empty cages were lined up along one wall.

There were stacks of order forms on the desk. I picked one up and saw that someone had ordered a falcon. That must be the bird that had lost its feather in the pet shop! And a falcon wasn't a normal pet. I thought about the animal shelter director's presentation at the pet show. She had talked about people illegally selling rare animals. Now I knew what Ziggy had been buying and selling in the library parking lot.

"Look out, Pinky!" Avi gasped. "It's a Gila monster!"

A giant lizard had crawled out from under the desk. "Nobody move," Madame Olga whispered. "Gila monsters have a terrible bite. They're poisonous!"

"I know what to do," Avi said. "Watch me tame the Gila monster."

He pulled out the whistle he'd bought to train his cockroaches. Then he blew into it as hard as he could.

The Gila monster must have heard the sound of the whistle. It stood still for a second, then slowly crawled back under the desk.

I didn't want to admit it, but at that moment, my little brother was my hero!

I breathed a sigh of relief. Then I started planning our escape.

I climbed on top of the desk so that I could reach the window. It was easy to open, and I was able to stick my head out. "Help!" I yelled. "We're locked inside the pet store!"

A familiar voice said, "Pinky Bloom? Is that you?"

Hannah Cohen was standing on the sidewalk. She set down the box she'd been holding and took out her cell phone.

"Hang in there!" she said. "I'm calling the police to come get you out."

A few minutes later, the door to the room opened, and an officer walked in. Hannah was right behind her.

I told the officer what was going on. "Ziggy has been selling all kinds of animals that aren't supposed to be pets. We interrupted one of his deals, and he locked us in here."

"We'll look into this," the officer said. She squinted at the floor. "Is that a Gila monster?"

Sure enough, the poisonous lizard was peeking out from under the desk again.

"It's illegal to keep Gila monsters as pets," said the officer. "Seems like you're right about what's been going on here, young lady."

"What's going to happen to Ziggy?" I asked.

"A judge will decide his punishment," she said. "And the pet store will have to pay a fine for illegally selling exotic animals."

"He was really mean to us," said Avi. "He told

me to put a sock in it. I guess *it* was my mouth, and the sock would block the sound of me talking."

I thought about what Avi had just said. Something that was blocking the sound . . .

"We have to get home!" I exclaimed. "I have a case to solve!"

Madame Olga chuckled. "It's never a dull moment with Pinky and Avi Bloom."

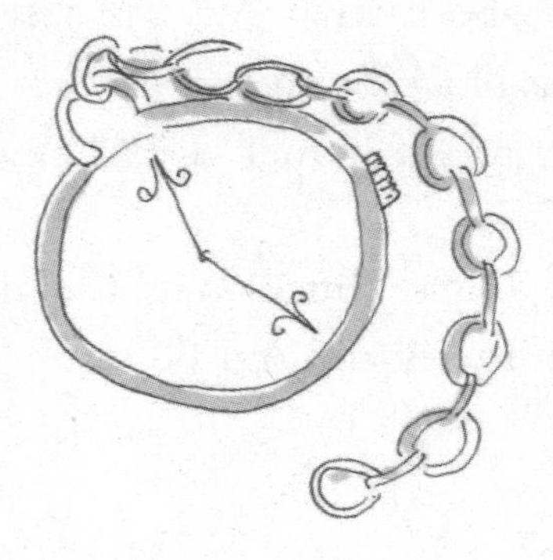

Chapter Nineteen

Officer Berman brought Avi and me home. Hannah came with us, since she had been on her way to bring Dad a new shofar when she'd heard me yelling from the pet store window.

"Thank you so much for helping the kids, Hannah," said Dad after we explained what happened. "And thanks for going to all this trouble to make the exchange. I'll go get the faulty shofar."

"I'll get it, Dad!" I said. This was the chance to prove my theory, and a metal clothes hanger was all I needed to do it.

A minute later, I stood in the middle of the living room. All eyes were on me as I held up the shofar. "I, Pinky Bloom, Brooklyn's greatest kid detective, will now unveil the shofar's secret."

I carefully threaded one end of the hanger into the shofar. With a twist of my wrist, I pulled out a pocket watch!

"This was blocking the sound," I said.

"But what is a pocket watch doing inside a shofar?" Dad demanded.

"Hannah put it there," I said. "The question is why."

Hannah hurried over and took the watch from me. "I can explain," she said. "This watch belonged to my great-grandfather, Harry Cohen. He was the original owner of the Judaica shop. He lost everything when he had to sell the store. But a few days ago, I came across the watch in the storage room. I really wanted to keep it, since it had been in my family."

"Mr. Simon sells a lot of Hebrew pocket watches," Dad said. "How do you know this one belonged to your great-grandfather?"

Hannah turned the watch over. Engraved on the back were the initials *H.C.*

"When I found it, I planned to tell Mr. Simon," she said. "But he was busy, so I hid the watch in the shofar for safekeeping until I could talk to him about it."

"How did my dad get that shofar?" I asked.

"It was by mistake," Hannah explained. "Mr. Simon brought this shofar out of the storage room to show Mr. Bloom. Then we were all distracted when Avi's cockroaches escaped. I meant to give Mr. Bloom the other shofar—the one he chose. But I mixed up the shofars, and instead he got the one with the watch inside."

"Well, I'm glad we got that straightened out," Grandma Phyllis said. "Now, Pinky, Avi, come eat dinner."

So Dad got his shofar, and Hannah left with her great-grandfather's pocket watch. After dinner, I went to my room and updated my detective note-book: *Case solved!*

Chapter Twenty

It had been a really long day. Solving a case had felt good, but Mei-Mei was still missing, and Lucy was coming to get her in the morning. How was I going to tell my best friend that I'd lost her pet? She might never forgive me.

I couldn't think straight when my room was such a mess. Most of the things scattered on the floor belonged to Avi. I was about to toss his backpack into my closet when I felt something moving around inside.

"Avi, what do you have in your backpack?"

"Nothing, Pinky. Just the snacks I brought for the cockroaches to eat at the picnic."

Mei-Mei poked her head out of the backpack. I lifted her out and covered her with kisses. "You were in here the whole time!" I cried.

"We never thought to look in my backpack," Avi said as I put Mei-Mei back in her cage and refilled her water bottle. "Good thing she was able to eat the food I packed for the cockroaches!"

For once, I was actually grateful for those cockroaches!

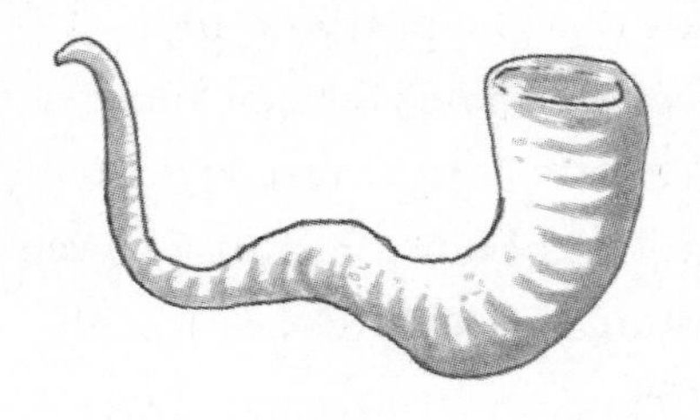

Chapter Twenty-One

The next morning, Lucy came by before school. "I hope you didn't have any trouble with Mei-Mei," she said.

I decided to wait awhile before I told her everything that had happened. For now, I just said, "I've realized that it's a big responsibility to take care of someone else's pet."

Then I told her what we'd discovered about the pet store. "Officer Berman has been keeping us up to date on the case. The police found a lot more animals in a storage locker that Ziggy owns. He was going to sell them all illegally."

"I guess some people will pay a lot of money for rare animals," said Lucy. "What's going to happen to the animals that the police found?"

"Officer Berman said that most of them will be sent to an exotic animal rescue center."

"Wow," said Lucy. "I think you need a new title: Pinky Bloom, Pet Rescuer!"

Rosh Hashanah got here before we knew it. At the synagogue, we proudly watched as Dad walked up to the bimah and held the shofar to his mouth.

"*Tekiah! Sh'varim! Teruah! Tekiah Gedolah!*" The blasts of the shofar came out loud and clear.

After services, my family and I wished our friends and neighbors a shana tova, "Happy New Year."

"A good year to you and your family, Pinky," said Madame Olga. "So how is the pet sitting business going? Maybe you'll watch Oy Vey when I go visit my sister on Long Island?"

"I'll be taking a break from pet sitting," I said. "Instead, I'm going to volunteer at the animal shelter!"

As a detective, I'd been trying to figure out what had gone so wrong with my pet sitting business. I'd decided that I needed more experience taking care of animals before I would be totally ready to look after other people's pets. So after the holidays, I went back to the shelter as a volunteer. And that's how I ended up adopting my very own guinea pig!

About the Author

Judy Press studied fine arts at Syracuse University and earned a master's in art education from the University of Pittsburgh. She is the creator of more than a dozen award-winning children's art activity books and early reader chapter books. A grandmother to ten, Press lives in Pittsburgh.

About the Illustrator

Erica-Jane Waters, originally from Ireland, credits her imagination to her childhood there and its wealth of folklore and fairy tales. She has been writing and illustrating children's books for over twenty years, using a mixture of traditional techniques and digital work to create her art. Waters lives in a 370-year-old tumbledown cottage in England with her husband and two children.